For Mums - hard-working heroes who never stop.

MZ

For Tom and Frank, no longer with us.

AW

Rita Wants a Witch published by Graffeg in 2021.
Copyright © Graffeg Limited 2021.

ISBN 9781802580402

First published by An tSnáthaid Mhór Teoranta 2018.

Text © Máire Zepf, illustrations © Andrew Whitson, design and production Graffeg Limited. This publication and content is protected by copyright © 2021.

Máire Zepf and Andrew Whitson are hereby identified as the authors of this work in accordance with section 77 of the Copyrights, Designs and Patents Act 1988.

A CIP Catalogue record for this book is available from the British Library.

Mae Rita Eisiau Gwrach (Welsh edition) ISBN 9781802580419
Ríta agus an Chailleach (Irish edition) ISBN 9781912929153

The publisher acknowledges the financial support of the Books Council of Wales. www.gwales.com

Teaching Resources
www.graffeg.com/pages/teachers-resources

1 2 3 4 5 6 7 8 9

This book belongs to

_____

_____

_____

_____

MIX
Paper from responsible sources
FSC
www.fsc.org
FSC® C014138

GRAFFEG

Rita
wants a Witch

By Máire Zepf

Illustrated by Mr Ando

This is Rita.

Rita loves Halloween.

Rita wants a witch.
A witch is wild-with-a-wand
and madly magical.

A witch would never make her go to bed on time, but let her fly around on a broomstick all night instead.

There would be
no need to clean

or to wash up
or to do homework.

Rita could help her to brew magic potions

and try out new spells.

A witch could cover a bully's face with oozy spots.

Or turn her teacher into a frog.

Teacher

Rita loves frogs.

Hopefully, her witch wouldn't be **too** spooky.

Because that could give Rita nightmares.

Or scare away her friends.

That would be terrible.

What if she didn't know what to do
when Rita was feeling unwell?

Or if she was mean and nasty,

and thought that Rita should be too?

That would be dreadful.

And would she want a kiss goodnight?
YUUUCK!

What if she only cooked
icky witchy food

for breakfast

lunch

and

dinner?

A witch could ruin everything.

And where would it end?

She doesn't want a witch after all.

Not a real one, anyway...